MONSTER MADNESS

MEGAN STINE & H. WILLIAM STINE

This book is dedicated to Cleveland.

Illustrations by Gordon Kibbee

ISBN 0-590-35181-8

12 11 10 9 8 7 6   4 5/9

CHAPTER 1

"Come on, Mickey. You will never catch a fish that way," Jan called to her friend. "You have got to hold on to the pole."

Jan sat at the edge of the lake holding her pole. Mickey's pole was sticking out from the ground. He sat under a tree reading a book.

"I don't need a pole to catch fish," Mickey called back. "This is my way of fishing. First, I get the fish to think I'm reading so they forget about me. Then, when they are not looking, I sneak up on them and pull them out of the water with my hands!"

"That is the dumbest thing I have ever heard," Jan said. But she was smiling.

"I don't know," Mickey said. "I still like the one about dressing up as a giant worm and scaring them out of the water. Anyway, let me finish this page. Then I'll do some real fishing."

"Well, what are you so busy reading?" Jan asked.

"Another monster book," Mickey answered. "It's about these monsters from Mars who come to Earth dressed as a baseball team. And then they try to win the World Series."

Jan was only half listening. She was looking

up into the black sky. "It's going to rain," she said to Mickey. "I think we had better head home."

Just then there was a loud clap of thunder. Mickey jumped to his feet. "It's going to pour!" he said. And just as he said it, lightning hit the ground.

"Let's get out of here!" Jan said, starting to run.

"What about the fishing poles?" Mickey called after her.

"Leave them! We can get them later."

"Wait," Mickey called. "I've got to get my lunch."

Jan turned around and came back. "Are you crazy?" she said. "Leave it."

"But I'm hungry. And it's my favorite sandwich," Mickey said.

But before he could reach for the brown paper bag, a bolt of lightning came down with a crack. It was a direct hit on the lunch bag. Jan and Mickey almost jumped out of their shoes. And then it happened. Mickey's sandwich started to grow.

First the paper bag tore open. And as Mickey and Jan moved away, the sandwich grew bigger and bigger. Soon it was over five feet long.

"I was hungry. But I wasn't that hungry," Mickey said.

It was impossible but it was happening. They couldn't believe their eyes. Now the sandwich was 10 feet long. The bread looked like a giant mattress.

Jan rubbed her eyes and said, "When is it going to stop?"

It was 20 feet long.

"Once they start growing, they never stop," Mickey said.

"Well, I'm not going to wait around to see," Jan said. "I think we had better get the Sheriff out here!"

Mickey and Jan headed for town. They stopped and looked back once to see if the sandwich was still growing. It was 30 feet long by then, almost as big as a house. After that, they didn't stop until they got to the Sheriff's door.

"Sheriff Richmond! Come quick!" Mickey said. "There is a giant sandwich out at the lake."

Sheriff Richmond sat at his desk. He was eating a plate of stew.

"What is the matter with you kids? Can't you see I'm busy?"

"But you are just eating your dinner," Jan said. "And there is a giant sandwich out at the lake!"

"I don't want a giant sandwich," the Sheriff said. "I want my plate of stew."

"But this sandwich is 30 feet long," Mickey said.

Sheriff Richmond looked at the book in Mickey's hand.

"You know, Mickey, I think you have been reading too many of those monster books. You are beginning to see things."

"I saw it too," Jan said. "Please come with us. It will only take a minute. You have got to see it."

Sheriff Richmond and a crowd of people from the town followed Mickey and Jan to the lake.

"Hurry," Jan told them all. "It must be 50 feet long by now."

"You kids had better be telling the truth," said the Sheriff.

"We are," Mickey said. "Just wait and see."

"We're almost there," Jan said. "So be careful because it might — " Jan stopped in the middle of her sentence. They had reached the lake, and the giant sandwich was gone.

CHAPTER 2

"I should lock you two up," the Sheriff said. "Right now!"

"Lock us up? What for?" Jan said.

"For making me miss my dinner. My stew must be ice cold by now."

"What is the matter with you two?" the deputy asked. "Don't you have anything better to do than to play jokes?"

"But...but...but...," Mickey tried to explain.

"Oh, be quiet, Mickey. You sound like a motor boat," the deputy said.

"We are not lying. Really. We saw a 30-foot sandwich. It was right here," Jan said.

"Well, maybe someone carried it away," the deputy said.

"That's right," Sheriff Richmond laughed. "Maybe it was a sandwich to go!"

"Well, I don't think it is funny. I say we see if their parents think it is funny," a man said.

Jan and Mickey did not say much as they slowly walked home.

"They think we are lying," Jan said.

"That is the way it always is in the books," Mickey said. "The sheriff never believes you at first."

"Well, what do you want to do?"

"There is only one thing to do," Mickey said.

"Right. We'll go back tomorrow. We'll be there when the sun comes up," Jan said.

There was still a chill in the air the next morning when they got to the lake. The sun was just beginning to come up. There was a thick white fog.

"It's too foggy to see," Jan said.

"Don't worry," Mickey said. "A 50-foot sandwich will not be too hard to spot. Are you scared?"

"Of course not," Jan said. "But I was just thinking. What if we do find it? What do we do then? We can't say, 'Put your hands up.'"

"Well, I have been looking through all my science fiction books. And the big mistake people make is they always think the monster is bad. Maybe the sandwich wants to make friends. Or maybe it is lonely."

"Or maybe it wants to join a baseball team."

"OK, don't make fun of my books," Mickey said. "They tell me a lot."

"Well, I'll tell you something. Even if the sandwich does want to be friends, don't ask it out to lunch." Jan stooped and picked up something from the ground under a tree.

"Very funny. Did you find something?"

"Nothing except this little green pickle from your lunch," Jan said. She skipped the pickle

across the lake like a stone. It made a ring where it sank.

"What's that?" Mickey said, pointing to something on the hill.

"It's a piece of lettuce," Jan said.

"Right. But it's as big as a living room rug," Mickey said. "That means the sandwich must be somewhere near."

They looked at each other, and then they looked at the hill.

"Well, let's go," Jan said.

They climbed the hill together and stood at the top.

"It must be somewhere around here," Mickey kept saying.

Then they saw it. Jan and Mickey held their breath. The sandwich was not lying on its side anymore. It was standing up on one end. And before they knew what was happening, the

50-foot sandwich started coming toward them.

They turned to run, but they could hardly take their eyes off the sandwich. They kept looking back as they ran down the hill.

"What do your books say to do?" said Jan.

"They say in a case like this: RUN FOR YOUR LIFE!"

And they did run. They ran as fast as they could. But the sandwich was right behind them.

CHAPTER 3

Mickey and Jan didn't stop running until they reached town. When they turned around to look, the sandwich was nowhere in sight.

"I think we lost it," Jan said.

"Let's get the Sheriff," Mickey said.

Mickey opened the door to the Sheriff's office and stepped in. The Sheriff was busy eating a plate of stew.

"Sheriff, Sheriff, come quick. It was chasing us!"

"Now what do you two want?" the Sheriff said, without looking up.

"The sandwich was chasing us," Jan said. "You have got to do something."

"You've got to believe us," Mickey said. "It stands on its end and runs real fast."

"If you two don't leave me alone, I'm going to stand you on your ends. Now get out of here before I lock you up."

"But Sheriff — " Mickey didn't get to finish the sentence.

"OUT!!"

"OK," Jan said. "But don't say we didn't warn you." Jan was angry. "Come on, Mickey."

"Grown-ups!" Jan said. "They wouldn't believe there was a wall in front of them until they ran into it."

"We have to get some proof," Mickey said. "And we had better find it before someone gets hurt."

"Well, there's no better proof than a photograph," Jan said.

"Great idea," Mickey said. "Let's go."

"Hold it a minute. Do you have a camera?"

"Uh, no," Mickey said. "Do you?"

"No. But I have the next best thing. I have a sister," Jan said.

"Swell," Mickey said. "You have a sister and I have dandruff. I don't see how either one is going to help."

"My sister works for the newspaper. She's a photographer. Get the picture?" Jan said with a smile.

The two of them burst in on Mary at the newspaper office. Mary was at her desk. Jan told her about the sandwich chasing them. But Mary didn't believe them any more than the Sheriff had.

"The least you can do is come with us to the lake," Jan said. "It will only take a minute. And if you get a picture of the sandwich, you can use it in the paper."

Mary didn't say anything.

"And besides," Jan added. "I did the dinner dishes all last week. So you owe me a favor."

"OK, OK. I'll go with you," Mary finally said.

"Great!" Mickey and Jan said.

Mary got her camera and followed them to the lake.

"Now we will show them," Jan said.

The lake was quiet, too quiet. It gave them all the creeps.

"Well, I don't see anything. I guess I'll be going," Mary said in a hurry.

"Wait a minute, Mary. You promised," Jan said.

"I know I promised. But the sandwich isn't here. I can't wait around all day, you know."

"But Mary, a 50-foot sandwich is not going to stand here and pose. We have got to look for it."

Mickey climbed over the hill.

"Where would you be if you were the world's biggest sandwich?" Jan asked.

"I would be in the world's biggest plastic bag," Mary said.

20

"It's not here," Mickey called from the hill.

"That's it. I'm leaving," Mary said.

Just then Mickey came running down the hill.

"Wait a minute. I found something," he said. His eyes were wide. "There is a huge trail on the other side of the hill. And it looks like a trail of mayonnaise."

Mickey looked up the hill. "I think we have to follow it," he said. "It's our only chance to prove that the sandwich exists."

The three of them stood there for a minute. They were all afraid of what they might find.

Mary brushed a speck of dust off her camera. "OK," she said finally. "We have to follow the trail, no matter where it might lead."

21

CHAPTER 4

The trail of mayonnaise was four feet wide. It led Mary, Jan, and Mickey through the woods and hills around the lake. At every turn, and down every hill, they thought they would find the sandwich. But they didn't.

"This isn't leading us anywhere," Mary said. "I think we are going in circles."

"It could be a trap," Mickey said. "I read in one book — "

"Shh. I hear something," Jan said.

The three of them listened. There was a strange sound in the air. It seemed to be coming from just over the next hill. Quietly the three climbed the hill and looked down. The sandwich was lying down again, but it was bigger than ever.

"It's resting," Jan said.

"I'm going to lean over to get a good picture," Mary said.

"No, don't," Jan said. "You might slip and roll down the hill."

"You'll have to hold me," Mary said. "But I've got to get closer."

Jan and Mickey held on to Mary as she leaned over. The sandwich was making funny noises. It

24

went "Gurgle, gurgle, gurgle." And with each gurgle it grew bigger.

"I can't believe how big it is," Mickey said. "I wonder why it is making so much noise?"

"Come on, you guys," Mary said. "Hold still. I keep shaking."

"That's because I keep shaking," Jan said. "Hurry up."

Just then Mary's foot slipped and sent some rocks rolling down the hill. The sandwich began snorting.

"I've got enough pictures," Mary said. "Let's get out of here."

Back at the newspaper Mary told her boss, "I've got something big — really big." Then she disappeared into the darkroom. Word got around fast. The whole town had heard. A crowd of people came to the office. They all waited to see Mary's pictures.

"Well, here they are," Mary said.

"Great pictures, Mary," Jan said.

"What's so great about a sandwich?" asked Mary's boss.

"Look closer," Mary said. "This sandwich is living in the woods. And it must be 50 feet long."

"Oh, no. Not again," Sheriff Richmond said. "I don't believe it. It's some kind of trick."

"No, it's not," Mary said. "I saw it!"

Sheriff Richmond got up and walked out. But Joe Sharp listened closely to every word. Joe Sharp was always trying to get rich quick. He was thinking hard about something. He moved closer to Jan and Mickey.

"A 50-foot sandwich is living in our woods?" Joe Sharp asked.

"Yes," Jan answered.

"And it's the truth," Mickey added.

"I believe you, my boy," Joe Sharp said. "Now tell me one thing: Just whose sandwich is it?"

"Well," Mickey said. "I guess it's mine."

"It's yours? It belongs to you?"

"Right. My mom made it for me."

"That's wonderful. My boy, how would you like to be rich? I mean richer than you have ever dreamed. It could happen, you know."

"How?"

"How?" Joe Sharp asked with a laugh. "Don't you see? We've got a gold mine here. People will come from all over the world to see this sandwich. And all we have to do is charge them to see it. We will be rich! You will be rich. I will make you rich. I will buy all the candy you want."

"My folks won't let me eat too much candy," Mickey said.

"Then I will buy you parents who will let you eat all the candy you want."

26

"I don't want new parents," Mickey said.

"OK, OK. But just think of it: You can have anything you want. All you have to do is leave everything to me. I will call the newspapers and the television stations. We will build a huge tent around the sandwich. We'll be rich. I'm telling you, my boy, this will be the greatest thing since sliced bread!"

CHAPTER 5

As they walked home, Jan could see Mickey was thinking about what Joe Sharp had said.

"Joe Sharp is always coming up with crazy ideas," Jan said.

"I know, but wouldn't it be great to have all that money?" Mickey said. "And at least he believes us. That's more than I can say for most people in this town."

"I guess you're right," Jan said.

All of a sudden they heard people screaming.

"What's going on?" Mickey asked.

"I don't know. You don't think it could be — " Jan didn't want to finish her sentence.

They ran in the direction of the noise. Jan was right. The sandwich was there. It was standing up and walking down the middle of the street. Women were screaming. Men were screaming. Everyone was running. The sandwich chased a couple of people, but only for a little way. Then it went back to walking through the town.

"Why does it keep turning from side to side?" Mickey asked.

"Maybe it's looking for something," Jan said.

Just then the sandwich stopped in its tracks. It

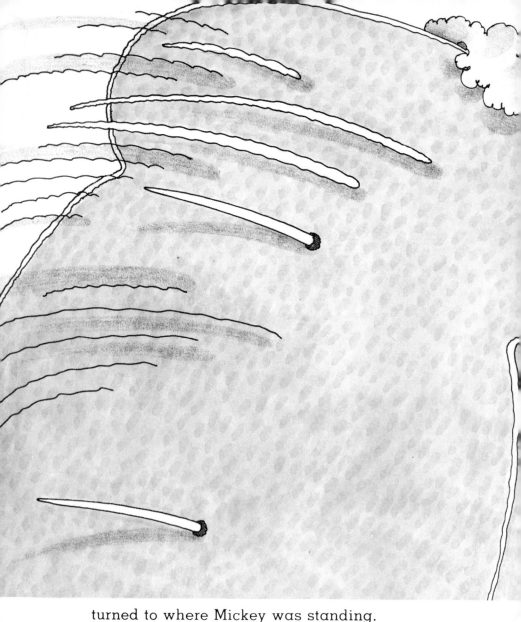

turned to where Mickey was standing.

"Mickey, it's turning toward you," Jan said. "I think it just found what it was looking for."

Mickey started moving away. The sandwich moved each time Mickey did. Giant tomato seeds fell to the ground as it walked.

"Help me, someone!" Mickey yelled, as he

took off down the street.

The sandwich moved faster and faster. It sounded as if it was breathing very heavily. Mickey tripped and fell just as a car screeched to a stop near him. It was Sheriff Richmond. He got out of his car and pointed his gun.

"OK, that's far enough," he called to the

sandwich. "You are under arrest."

The sandwich kept coming.

"You have the right to remain silent," Sheriff Richmond said. "And you have the right to talk to a lawyer."

The sandwich kept coming.

"OK, you. Up against the car."

The sandwich walked over to the car and stomped it to the ground.

"You can't do that. I still owe money on it!"

Sheriff Richmond yelled.

The sandwich turned around and started to walk toward them.

"OK, you asked for it," the Sheriff said.

He fired a shot, but the bullet went right through a hole in the Swiss cheese. He fired again, and this time the sandwich turned and ran. It seemed to be headed back to the lake and the hills.

Jan came running up to Mickey and the

Sheriff. "Mickey! Are you all right?" Jan asked.

"I think so," Mickey said. His voice was very quiet. "Thanks, Sheriff."

"That's OK. And I guess I owe you kids an apology."

Just then Joe Sharp came out of the crowd and walked over to them. "See, I told you this was the best thing that ever happened to this town," Joe Sharp said.

"It's not the best thing that ever happened to my car," Sheriff Richmond said.

"Your car? You'll be able to buy a hundred cars when people start pouring into town."

"Look, Joe. We have got to put that sandwich out of business before someone gets hurt. It seems to want Mickey."

"Love — that's what it is. The sandwich knows its owner. It loves Mickey."

"I'm not too sure about that," Sheriff Richmond said. "I'm forming a posse. Any of you men want to help me track down the sandwich?"

No one said a word.

"Well, how about any of you women?"

No one said a word.

"Any children? I'll take children and dogs . . . anyone?"

No one said a word.

"All right," the Sheriff said. "I'll do it myself. That's the thanks I get, after all I've done for this town!"

"Well, OK, I'll go with you." It was the Sheriff's deputy.

Finally some other people said they would go also.

"Good," Sheriff Richmond said. "We will take care of this sandwich once and for all."

"But Sheriff," Joe Sharp said. "I beg you. Bring it back alive."

CHAPTER 6

Everyone gathered in the newspaper office to plan an attack. Mickey and Jan called their parents. They came to the office right away. The room buzzed with everyone talking at once. And everyone was talking about the same thing — the sandwich.

"I can't believe it," Mickey's mother said. "The sandwich I made?"

"No one believed us. That's why we didn't tell you before. We had to get proof," Jan explained.

"Well, one thing is for sure," Mickey's father said. "This is one recipe no one will ask you for."

"OK folks, quiet down," Sheriff Richmond was trying to say over the noise. "Quiet, please. Now, as most of you know, we have got a real problem. There is a 50-foot sandwich living in our woods. Now we are going out there to try to do something about it. It's going to be a little tricky — mostly because we don't know what to do."

"I know what to do," someone in the crowd said. "We should just leave the sandwich alone. In a few weeks it will go stale."

"We can't wait a few weeks," another man

said. "We've got to do something now. It will kill us. It will ruin our appetites."

"Friends," Mickey's mother said. "I think we are going about this all wrong. You are thinking about this thing as a sandwich. But we should be thinking about it as a monster — a monster we have got to destroy."

"Wait a minute — not so fast!" Joe Sharp rushed to the front of the room. "You can't do that. Don't you see? You can't think of that sandwich as a monster. You have got to think of it as a television star."

"What???" everyone in the room said.

"That's right. I have a great idea for a TV show. We will be rich and famous!"

"What kind of show can a sandwich star in?" Sheriff Richmond asked.

"A cowboy show, of course," Joe Sharp said. "It will be called 'The Sandwich That Brought Law and Order to the West.' There are a few problems, of course. Like how to find a horse big enough for the sandwich to ride. But I'm sure I can work out all the small details."

"Joe," said the Sheriff, "I don't know who is crazier — you for talking, or us for listening."

Just then the deputy came into the room. "OK, Sheriff. We're all set."

"Good, then we are ready. Come on, Jan and Mickey. You two have to show us where the

sandwich is hiding."

Most of the town followed them out to the lake. The deputy drove a pick-up truck.

"What is in the truck?" people asked.

"You will see. It's not much, but it's the best we can do right now."

When the crowd reached the lake, Mickey and

Jan stepped forward. "Well, it should be just over the hill," Mickey said.

The deputy crept over the hill, took a look, and came back down.

"It's down there, all right," he said. "And I think it's asleep."

"Good," the Sheriff said. "I need some of you people to help me at the truck."

Everyone crowded around to see what was in the truck. The Sheriff pulled out a giant net, some stakes, and some pieces of rope.

"If we tie it down, we can control it," the Sheriff said. "Then at least it won't be able to hurt anyone."

They slowly and quietly crept down the hill. "Now!" Sheriff Richmond called. The net was thrown over the sandwich. The sandwich moved a little in its sleep.

"Now put those stakes through the net and drive them into the ground."

When the last stake had been driven in, the Sheriff ordered them to take the ropes and tie the net to the stakes. In a matter of minutes the sandwich was trapped.

"Well, the sandwich didn't put up much of a fight," he said. "It hardly moved at all. Do you think it's already dead?"

It was right then that the sandwich let out a tremendous roar.

CHAPTER 7

The sandwich roared once again. The sandwich roared so loud that the people had to hold their ears. Then, to everyone's surprise, the sandwich spoke.

"Humans," the sandwich said. It had a big, deep voice. And it rumbled when it talked.

"You are cruel and mean to your sandwiches. And I am going to destroy you!"

The sandwich twisted and turned under the net. It roared again. Everyone backed away.

"I am the sandwich who will rule the world," the sandwich roared. "If you don't listen to me, I will tear down every house in your town. Now is the time for all sandwiches to stand up on their own two crusts!"

The sandwich was quiet for a minute. Sheriff Richmond moved closer to it. He could see the sandwich's middle moving up and down. It looked as if it was breathing hard.

"Listen, humans, and listen carefully," the sandwich said. Sheriff Richmond had to back away again.

"These are my demands. You must do what I say. And you must do it now.

"1. No more mashing the bread when you butter it.

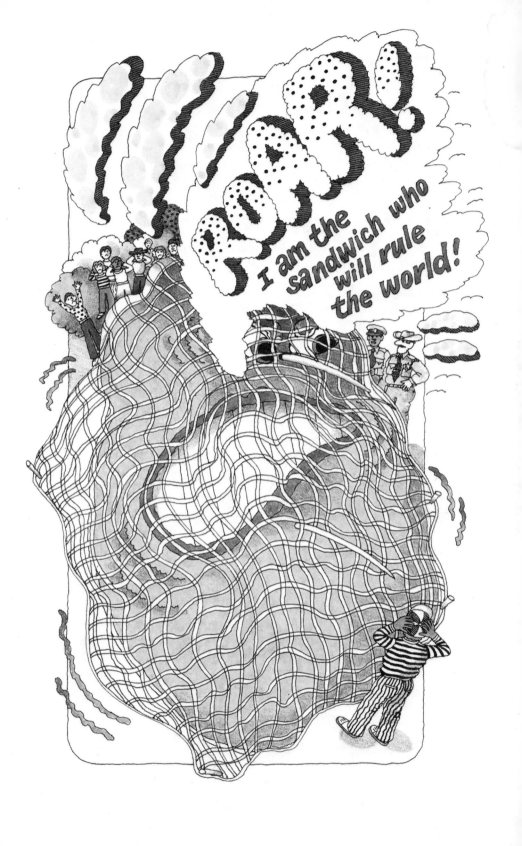

"2. No more cutting the crust off to make small sandwiches.

"3. Stop all weird combinations like sardines and peanut butter."

All these demands were hard to take. Besides, no one was used to taking orders from a sandwich. But the sandwich was still not satisfied. It spoke again.

"And that's not all!" the sandwich roared. "There is one more thing I must have."

Everyone held his breath, waiting to hear what the sandwich would say.

"Some hungry boy wanted to eat me," the sandwich said. "But I will have my revenge! I am going to eat him!"

The crowd gasped. Mickey's mother grabbed him and held on.

"It must be crazy," people shouted. "The sandwich is crazy."

"GIVE ME THE BOY WHO WAS GOING TO EAT ME," the sandwich shouted, "OR I WILL DESTROY YOUR TOWN!"

"What can we do?" people asked Sheriff Richmond. The Sheriff walked up and down, thinking.

"I have an idea," someone said. "What spoils a sandwich faster than burning the toast?"

"I see what you mean," the deputy said. "If we can get some flame throwers, we can burn

45

that sandwich to a crisp."

"I guess it's worth a try," the Sheriff said. The deputy went off to look for the tools. A few minutes later he came back with the flame throwers.

"OK, let him have it," the Sheriff called out.

The flame throwers made a tremendous noise. But above the noise of the flame throwers, they could hear the sandwich roar. A

few parts turned brown. But it was the net that burst into flames. And in a moment the ropes burned too.

"I am free!" the sandwich shouted in a deep, angry voice. It stood up and towered above the crowd. "I'm going to run around and work up an appetite. Then I am going to eat that boy!"

The sandwich made a sound that was like a laugh. Then it ran off, growling, into the woods.

CHAPTER 8

Later that day, Sheriff Richmond went to Mickey's house.

"Well, Mickey, it's too bad the flame throwers burned the net. It's too bad the sandwich got away."

Mickey was quiet for a while. "Sheriff, I don't want to give myself up to the sandwich. But what are we going to do?"

"That's what I came to talk about, Mickey. Where are your folks?"

"They are in the living room," Mickey said. "My mom won't stop crying because she thinks it's all her fault. She says she won't ever set foot in the kitchen again. She is afraid to bake a cake because it might try to take over the world. I wish you'd tell her to stop blaming herself."

"I'll do what I can, Mickey."

The Sheriff walked into the living room. Mickey's mother and father were sitting there with the lights out.

"You can't have my boy," Mickey's father told the Sheriff.

"If the sandwich wants me to, I'll bake it a nice gingerbread boy. But it can't eat my son," Mickey's mother said.

"I'm not going to let it eat anyone," the Sheriff said. "But I do need your help. I want you to tell me exactly what is in the sandwich you made. Then maybe we can figure out a plan."

"Well, it's a delicious sandwich. It's Mickey's favorite," his mother explained. "First you toast the bread — not too light and not too dark. Then you butter — "

"Please," the Sheriff interrupted. "I really don't have time for a recipe. Just tell me what is in the sandwich."

"Well, it has butter, mayonnaise, ham, turkey, Swiss cheese, tomato, and lettuce. And I also stuck a couple of toothpicks in it to keep it together. That's all I remember. Is that what you wanted to know?"

"Yes, it is, exactly. And I think I have an idea.

But I will need your help."

"What do you mean?" Mickey's father asked.

Just then Mickey and Jan came into the room.

"I'm glad you are here, Mickey. I want you to hear this," the Sheriff said. "I want to use Mickey as a decoy. I want to pretend we are giving him to the sandwich."

"NO!" his parents said.

"It's not really as dangerous as it sounds," the Sheriff said.

"It's OK, Mom," Mickey said. "If it's a good plan, I don't think we have a choice. I mean, this is just like the book I read, THE MONSTER WITH THE BIG GREEN EYES. They used a person as a decoy to get the monster to come out of hiding."

"Well, OK," his mother said. "But you had better make sure that nothing goes wrong."

The Sheriff promised.

Then Mickey and Jan said they were going to the newspaper office. "They want to interview us," Jan said. "We will be back in a little while."

When they got to the office, Joe Sharp came out of the crowd to hug Mickey.

"There you are, my boy. You know, folks, I've been like a father to this boy."

"Mr. Sharp, you never even spoke to me until yesterday," Mickey said.

"Uh, that's what I mean. I've been like a long

lost uncle to this boy. Now, my boy, tell the reporters about the great new cookbook we have planned."

"I don't know what you are talking about," Mickey said.

Joe Sharp laughed a big, nervous laugh.

"What a kidder this boy is. Always making jokes. Well that's all right. I'll tell them. We are writing a cookbook with a picture of the sandwich on the cover. I'm calling it BIG SANDWICHES FOR BIG MOUTHS. It will have lots of big recipes. It will be great, I tell you. We will be rich!"

Everyone in the room was laughing at Joe Sharp and having a good time. Mary took lots of pictures. And before Mickey could worry about tomorrow, it was time to go home and to bed.

CHAPTER 9

The next day the Sheriff picked up Mickey and his parents. The Sheriff was driving an old, beat-up car.

"It's embarrassing — the Sheriff of the town driving a junky car like this. But after what happened to my good car, I am not going to take any chances."

The Sheriff was trying to make everyone think about other things. But it didn't work too well. Everyone could think only about the sandwich eating Mickey. Jan held his hand. They had been friends for a long time, but this was the first time she had ever done that.

"You know what I did this morning?" she asked Mickey.

"No, what?"

"I cut off the crusts of every piece of bread in the house. No sandwich is going to tell me what to do."

There was a big crowd at the lake. Everyone looked sad.

Joe Sharp came up to them when they got out of the car. He held out his hand for Mickey to shake.

"I just want you to know that it's been nice

knowing you. After all, it's not everyone who gets a chance to be eaten by his own lunch. I just wish I were a few years younger. Then it would be me going out there to face that sandwich."

"Sure, Mr. Sharp," Mickey said.

"OK, folks. I would like to have a few words with Mickey," the Sheriff said. He put his arm around Mickey and took him aside.

"Mickey, here is all you have to do. Just sit by the lake and pretend to read a book. OK? If the sandwich doesn't come out, say something to make it mad. And leave the rest to me."

"What are you going to do?" Mickey asked.

"Well, if I told you, you would think I was crazy. So you will just have to trust me. Besides, we will be close by in case something goes wrong. You ready?"

"I guess so."

Mickey walked over to the tree and sat down under it. He looked around but he saw nothing. Still, he had the feeling he was being watched. Mickey opened his book and tried to read. But he couldn't keep his mind on the words. Finally he said in a loud voice:

"I sure am hungry. Boy am I hungry. And you know what I would like to eat? A sandwich. A big juicy sandwich."

Mickey heard noises coming from the woods.

They were getting louder and closer. So Mickey talked a little more.

"Yes, sir, there is nothing I would like better than to be eating a sandwich right now. Sandwiches are my favorite food to eat."

With a roar, the sandwich burst out of the woods.

"OK, Sheriff, it's here!" Mickey called. "You can come out now. Sheriff Richmond? Can you

hear me? Sheriff Richmond???"

The sandwich was bigger than Mickey had remembered. He could just see over the top of the sandwich as it moved toward him.

"OK, Sheriff, it's time for your plan. You don't have to wait anymore. It's here... and it's going to eat me!"

Mickey could hear strange noises coming from the sandwich. They sounded like a stomach rumbling with hunger. The sandwich moved closer, so Mickey took a step back. He looked everywhere. But Sheriff Richmond was nowhere in sight.

Mickey stepped back so far that he walked into the lake up to his ankles.

"Sheriff!!"

Then Mickey heard whirling noises in the sky. He looked up and saw a helicopter flying over his head. It was coming down fast, but the sandwich was coming closer. Finally the helicopter came close enough for Mickey to see it well. There was a man hanging down from it on a rope. Just as the sandwich moved toward Mickey, the man on the rope grabbed the sandwich's toothpicks. He pulled the toothpicks out, and the helicopter flew away.

The sandwich made one last roar before the bread fell open. All the lettuce, cheese, and meats slipped out and crashed to the ground.

CHAPTER 10

For a minute the sandwich tried to pull itself together. But all the power had gone out of it — as well as all the tomatoes, cheese, and meats. So it just lay there. And then it started to get smaller.

Everyone came rushing up to Mickey. They slapped him on the back and shook his hand. His parents hugged him. But Mickey just watched the sandwich until it was back to normal size. Then Mickey smiled. The crowd picked him up and carried him back to town on their shoulders.

"You did a good job," Sheriff Richmond told Mickey. "Sorry it was so close. But when I called for the helicopter and told them what I wanted it for, they thought I was crazy. But finally they believed me."

"I feel as if I've just lost a million dollars," Joe Sharp said. "And all because of you, Mickey. There goes my TV show, and my cookbook, and my radio."

"Your radio? What radio?" Mickey asked.

"The one shaped like a giant sandwich. Push one button and you get music. Push another button and you get mayonnaise. I would have been rich."

"Joe Sharp, you are the greediest man I know," Mickey's mother said.

"I am not. Besides, I only wanted the money for the orphans in town."

"But there are no orphans in this town," Mickey said.

"Oh," Joe Sharp said and walked away.

That night, Mickey and his family were watching the news. They couldn't believe it when a picture of the Sheriff eating a plate of stew came on.

"Here is a story you won't believe," the newswoman said. "Sheriff Richmond reported today that his town was under attack by a 50-foot sandwich. Yes, you heard me right, a 50-foot sandwich. He says the sandwich was destroyed earlier today so there is no danger. The Sheriff said the sandwich belonged to Mickey Albert who reads a lot of monster books. I don't know about you folks, but I find this story a little hard to swallow. In other news —— "

Mickey turned off the TV.

"Well, it is pretty hard to believe," his father said.

"I guess so," Mickey said.

The phone rang. It was Jan.

"Did you see the news?" she asked.

"Yes," Mickey answered.

"Well, you said they never believe the people in the books."

"You're right," Mickey said.

"You want to do something tomorrow, Mickey?"

"Sure, what? You want to go fishing?"

"Well," Jan said. "I'll tell you. I don't feel much like going fishing for a while. You know what I mean?"

"Sure," Mickey said.

"Do you want to go to the library? You could get some more books."

"No," Mickey said. "I'm giving up monster books."

"You are?" Jan sounded surprised. "Why?

Because of the sandwich?"

"No, because I've read them all. But I've got this great book about a parrot. He calls up girls and makes dates with them. Then he flies over to pick them up. Anyway, I thought we could go to the pet store. Do you think I can teach a parrot to dial a telephone, Jan . . . Jan? Hello, Jan . . .?"

Mickey heard a click. No one was on the other end of the line.

"It sounds like a great idea to me," Mickey said to himself. And he went to his room to finish the book.

The lights burned late in town that night. Everyone stayed up talking about what had happened. But, one by one, the lights went out. The town went to sleep feeling safe and happy.

No one knew — no one even dreamed — that right in the middle of the lake, growing bigger and bigger, there was an enormous 50-foot pickle.